Good Night, Veronica

By the same authors

RABBIT COUNTRY
THE ROYAL HICCUPS

Good Night, Veronica

Story and Pictures by Denise and Alain Trez

The Viking Press   New York

For V. V. V.
this story of Veronica

Translated from the French by Douglas McKee. Copyright
© 1968 by Denise and Alain Trez. All rights reserved. First
published in 1968 by The Viking Press, Inc. 625 Madison
Avenue, New York, N.Y. 10022. Published simultaneously in
Canada by The Macmillan Company of Canada Limited.
Library of Congress catalog card number: 68–18121. Printed
in U.S.A. by Neff Lithographing Company.
Pic Bk 1. Nonsense Stories

One night it was so hot that Veronica could not sleep. Her dog, Citron, snored peacefully beside her bed, but Veronica tossed and turned and longed for a breath of cool air…

so naturally she felt much better when she found herself abed high up in a tree in the garden. But not Citron! He felt airsick, and shook so much that

they both fell to the ground. That upset the tree, and it ran away. "How shall we ever find our way home without it?" Veronica cried.

On a big rock she wrote the word WANTED, and under it she drew a picture of the tree. Just then it began to rain...

and soon it was raining so hard that fish swam through the air. Veronica and Citron ran to take shelter in a woods.

By the time the rain stopped, they were completely lost. But Veronica
spied a long string on the ground. She began following it, rolling it up
as she went along.

To her surprise she discovered that it came from a big cloud that was unraveling like a sweater. "So the clouds are made of wool," Veronica said to Citron. "Maybe that's why they look like sheep!"

The cloud, which was now a small one, looked so white and cool that Veronica couldn't resist jumping into it.

Luckily the rain had made the plants grow so much that they made a ladder for her to get back down.

Veronica and Citron found themselves in a strange garden full of astonishing plants.

"Look, Citron," said Veronica, "Here's your chance to learn to read."

But Citron didn't like reading. He ran away and while Veronica was looking

for him, a giant shadow appeared on the ground. Was it the shadow of a bird?

Yes, it was! An egg fell on Veronica's head.

If it was a magic bird, Veronica wanted to see it up close. She ran after it, not knowing that her hair, too, had grown long in the rain. She soared into the air.

16

But the bird vanished over the horizon and Veronica came down to earth in her own parachute.

Fortunately, Citron recognized her long hair, spreading out like a country lane, and followed it back to her.

"I can make my hair grow as long as I wish," Veronica told Citron. "And see, I can stretch my arm to pick that apple."

It was even more fun to cross a river. Citron was amazed,

but he pretended he wasn't. He began to lap up the river water.

Now it was Veronica's turn to be amazed.

Citron began to shrink. He became smaller

and smaller until he was only a tiny little dog.

Veronica tried to comfort him, although she rather liked him that size. He won't eat so much, she said to herself.

Suddenly a rhinoceros who had been drinking at the river saw Veronica.
He charged at her, full of fury, and Veronica was terrified.

But he, too, began to shrink. By the time he reached her, Veronica could pick him up in her arms.

Many other animals came to the river to drink, and soon Veronica had a whole zoo of them. An elephant, a lion and a tiger, a camel, an antelope, and a giraffe—all as small as bunnies.

Then out of nowhere came a giant snail. "Look out!" shouted Citron.
"Snails don't drink river water!" He rushed to Veronica's defense, and
was so full of courage that he became his normal size again.

Everything was so odd that Veronica and Citron began to wish that they were safe at home. But where was home? Veronica was surprised to see her reflection in the water point a certain way... toward a curious tree.

"Let's rest a minute," said Veronica, "and watch TV."

Not far away, they found their own tree, sitting patiently and waiting for them.

Veronica opened the door, and she and Citron walked right in and up the stairs.

A few minutes later they were tucked away in their room. It was still dark and there was still time to sleep.

Good night, Citron! Good night, Veronica!